A sloth bear cub.

Having a Family

Bears are big animals when grown up, but they are born very small. Northern bears give birth in the den to cubs that weigh less than a pound. An American black bear cub, for example, weighs only 8½ to 11½ ounces (240 to 330 grams) at birth. That's like a human mother giving birth to a baby the size and weight (5 ounces, or 142 grams) of a wren. In fact, human babies normally weigh at least 5 pounds (2.27 kilograms).

Polar-bear cubs grow fast on their mother's rich milk.

Bears usually have from one to three cubs. The cubs are born blind, almost hairless, and completely helpless. But while in the den, they grow fast on their mother's milk, which can contain 33 percent fat. By the time the family leaves the den, the cubs have plenty of thick, fluffy fur, bright curious eyes, and a spirit of adventure.

The cubs stay with their mother for at least several months. In the Far North, brown bear cubs may live with their mothers for three years before they know enough to survive on their own.

CHAPTER THREE

North American Bears

As mentioned earlier, three kinds of bears—polar bears, brown (grizzly) bears, and American black bears—live in North America. The first two kinds also live in other parts of the Northern Hemisphere. Only the American black bear is found on the North American continent and nowhere else.

The Most Familiar Bear

The American black bear (*Ursus americanus*) lives in forests from Alaska and northern Canada all the way south into Mexico and Florida. It roams the forests of Washington and Maine. It is found in more places in North America than other bears and in greater numbers. Even so, few people are lucky enough to see a wild black bear. These animals generally live among the trees and stay away from people. Only when they learn that humans have food do they lose their shyness. Then they can be dangerous.

An American black bear.

The name, black bear, can be very confusing, since these animals cover a range of color all the way from black to white. They got their name because bears in the eastern United States, where the early settlers lived, were almost all black, with brown eyes and muzzles. But farther west, many black bears are brown. The bluish "glacier bear" is a black bear living in the Saint Elias mountains of Alaska. The rare cream, yellow, or orangish Kermode bear lives along Canada's north-western coast.

Black bears are the smallest kind living in North America. An average adult is 35 to 40 inches (89 to 102 centimeters) at the shoulder when standing on all fours and 4½ to 6 feet (1.37 to 1.82 meters) tall when standing on its hind legs. They can weigh from 125 to more than 600 pounds (57 to 272 kilograms). Male black bears are larger than the females by about a third.

A wild black bear in Montana.

This blond grizzly lives in Denali National Park in Alaska. Notice the hump on the top of its shoulders.

The Great Brown Bear

Grizzly bear is the name we give in much of North America to the brown bear (*Ursus arctos*). The brown bear is the most successful species of bear around the world. Its range includes most of the Northern Hemisphere, where it lives both in forests and across the treeless tundra.

Like the black bear, the brown bear is misnamed. Its color can range from black to shades of brown all the way to blond, or a mixture of colors. Brown bears are very strong. Their bodies are chunky, with a hump of muscle and fat on top of their shoulders. Their heads are big and they have very powerful jaws. Their paws are armed with long, thick claws. Despite their bulk, brown bears can sprint as fast as 35 miles per hour (56 kilometers per hour), which allows them to run down elk calves and other prey.

The size of brown bears can be different, depending on where they live. A typical bear in Yellowstone National Park might weigh 400 pounds (182 kilograms). Brown bears in parts of southern Europe are small, averaging only 154 pounds (70 kilograms), about the weight of an adult human. The biggest brown bears live along far northern coastlines, such as on Kodiak Island, where they can feed on salmon.

The grizzly cubs watch as their mother waits patiently for salmon to swim by.
DOROTHY H. PATENT

◀
You can get a sense of
how big polar bears are
in this photo of a captive
bear in a zoo.

▶
The paws of polar bears
are especially adapted for
walking on snow and ice.

The Polar Bear

Polar bears (*Ursus maritimus*) are different from other bears
in many ways. While most bears can live in many environ-
ments, polar bears are only found in the Far North, mostly on
the arctic ice. Scientists think the polar bear developed from
brown bears during the Ice Age that occurred 25,000 to
100,000 years ago.

The hairs of the polar bear's thick, creamy white coat are
hollow. The hollow hairs carry warmth from the sun's rays
directly to the bear's body, helping to warm it. Their fore-
paws can be a foot (30.5 centimeters) in diameter and have
webbed toes that act like snowshoes on land and paddles in
the frigid water. The thick fur on the bottoms of their feet
helps keep them from slipping on the ice.

CHAPTER FOUR

Bears in Today's World

Bears are very powerful animals that may use their size and strength to get what they want. They can be dangerous if they learn people are a good source of food. When people were allowed to feed bears in parks, the animals sometimes damaged cars or hurt people in their search for something to eat.

Nowadays, visitors to parks like Yellowstone feel lucky if they even see a bear in the distance. We have learned that it is better both for bears and for people if the animals don't get fed by us. They need to be allowed to stay wild, hunting for food in the forests and meadows instead of in garbage dumps and along roadsides.

Bears can get into trouble with people when they get too close.

Bears in Trouble

Most kinds of bears are having trouble surviving in today's crowded world. Almost all bears are being forced from their homes as people take over the land. Bears have already had to leave from 50 to 75 percent of the land where they once lived. Every day, more and more bear habitat is destroyed.

The closer people move to wild places, the more conflicts with bears occur. The spectacled bear is unpopular in South America because it raids croplands and beehives. The grizzly sometimes kills sheep or injures hikers. The sun bear is hunted in Indonesia when it damages crops. Other bears have the same kinds of conflicts with people.

People sometimes kill bears for their hides. In addition, bear gallbladders and other organs are used in Asian medicine. Young bears are also captured to be raised as pets, and their mothers are often killed.

A Malayan sun bear.

The sloth bear is better off than other Asian bears because of its limited range and specialized feeding habits that don't conflict with people.

Saving Asian Bears

The Asian bears are all losing ground. Laws that protect bears are hard to enforce in the countryside. As humans spread across the land, more space is set aside for croplands and towns. This means less land for bears and other wildlife.

Conservationists, people who work toward helping wildlife survive, are trying to solve these problems. For example, conservation groups are working with the Chinese government to try to save the giant panda. They want to stop hunters from killing bears and are working to set aside enough forestland for the pandas to live in.

Bringing Back Bears

Not all bears are in trouble today. Polar bears are protected in the five countries in which they live. At present, their numbers don't seem to be getting any smaller. But oil and gas development in the Arctic could cause problems for polar bears.

There are more American black bears now than there were fifty years ago, especially in the eastern United States. The bear population of Pennsylvania has doubled to around 7,000 since the 1970s, while New York has around 4,100 black bears. Out west, anywhere from 30,000 to 60,000 black bears roam Washington State.

American black bears seem to be doing all right.

While grizzlies are having a hard time in the lower forty-eight states, they are abundant in Alaska, where this grizzly family forages for food.

Conservationists are also working at bringing back grizzly bear populations in the lower forty-eight states, but it is not easy. Only recently, grizzlies in Yellowstone National Park seem to be recovering.

Saving bears from extinction is a difficult task. But it can be done if the people of the world learn to value these powerful animals and the wild places where they live.

Bears of the World

Bears belong to the scientific family Ursidae. The family is divided further into three subfamilies. Here are the bears of the world and where they are found.

SUBFAMILY TREMARCTINAE

Tremarctos ornatus   The spectacled bear—parts of South America.

SUBFAMILY URSINAE

Ursus thibetanus   The Asiatic black bear—many parts of Asia.

Ursus americanus   The American black bear—over much of North America.

Ursus arctos   The brown, or grizzly, bear—various areas across the Northern Hemisphere.

Ursus maritimus   The polar bear—the arctic region.

Ursus malayanus   The Malayan sun bear—parts of east and Southeast Asia.

Ursus ursinus   The sloth bear—India, Nepal, Bangladesh, and Sri Lanka.

SUBFAMILY AILUROPODINAE

Ailuropoda melanoleuca   The giant panda—central China.

Index

(numbers in italics refer to pages with photos)